con

Suzuki, Goodbye

Sam McBratney

Illustrated by
Peter Dennis

CollinsEducational
An imprint of HarperCollins*Publishers*

Published by Collins Educational
77-85 Fulham Palace Road, London W6 8JB.

© HarperCollins*Publishers*

ISBN 0 00 323050 3

Sam McBratney asserts the moral right to be identified as
the author of this work.

Reprinted 1996, 2000

llustration and page layout by Peter Dennis
Cover design by Clinton Banbury
Cover illustration by Peter Dennis

Commissioning Editor: Domenica de Rosa
Editors: Rebecca Lloyd and Paula Hammond
Production: Mandy Inness

www.**Collins**Education.com
On-line Support for Schools and Colleges

Printed and bound in Great Britain by Omnia Books Ltd, Glasgow

Suzuki, Goodbye

Contents

Chapter 1
See How She Runs

The blue Suzuki was nearly four years old, but it didn't look its age. It looked like a new bike.

The three people in the garage were Bill, his sister Caroline, and their friend John.

Bill was saying goodbye to the Suzuki. The bike belonged to his dad and it was up for sale.

BLUE Suzuki for sale, lovely condition. Good price for quick sale. Tel. 0412 2641

Caroline was not sorry that her dad was selling his bike. He would be a lot safer if he bought a car and had four wheels under him instead of just two. Her mum often called that motorbike a death-trap.

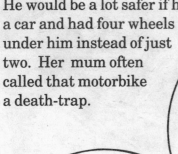

3

John got up on the Suzuki. He lay along the tank and made vroom-vroom noises out of the side of his mouth.

He leaned to one side to skim round an imaginary corner. But he leaned over too far.

The bike did a wobbly, threw its rider to the stone floor, and toppled over with a horrible clatter.

Actually, the motorbike had only suffered a dent in the petrol tank and a cracked wing mirror.

Caroline helped the boys to lift the bike upright. All this proved yet again that bikes were dangerous monsters. You could even crash one while it was standing still!

When their dad came home he had one or two things to say about fools who couldn't even sit on a bike without falling off it – but he accepted that Bill hadn't done the damage. He was quite fair that way.

After tea a man called at the front door. He wanted to see the bike. Bill followed them out to the garage to hear the chat.

As the men talked money, Bill looked at the stranger. He had a black beard and silver-framed glasses. The crash helmet he carried was red and yellow.

The stranger put on his helmet. He wanted to take the bike for a run so that he could listen to the engine.

The engine kicked sweetly into life. The stranger rode
to the end of the street, where he turned right towards
the city centre and disappeared from view.

Bill and his dad waited for him to come back. Bill
could see his dad getting more and more angry. And
he thought he knew the reason why.

9

That evening, Bill phoned John to tell him the news.

A man came and stole the bike. He just rode away on it and never came back. You should see dad – he's going bananas.

What did he look like? Was he young or old? What colour was his helmet? Did he have any missing teeth when he smiled...?

Bill knew what John was thinking. It would be great to find that ratbag and get the Suzuki back. Was such a thing possible?

Where would you even start?

Chapter 2
Walking the Plank

Raymond Chance was the stranger's name. The morning after he rode away on the blue Suzuki, he looked in the mirror above his workbench. He tapped his beard and put on his silver glasses.

What do you think?

Perfect.
I hardly know you.

Chance and his apprentice, Derek, jumped into a grey, unmarked van. Chance was driving.

Raymond Chance had a garage near the river. He fixed motorcycles for a living. There wasn't much money in small repair jobs, so he also bought and sold used bikes. This helped to raise some of the money he needed for racing at the weekends.

It had always been his dream to race bikes – "chasing rainbows" his old man used to call it. The old man had wanted him to work in a shop.

Chance hoped to find a sponsor who would back him on the race track with *real* money. In the meantime, when he needed a little extra cash, he stole a motorbike and sold it. This was highly illegal of course. But it brought the rainbow a little closer.

Slowly, Chance drove the grey van up and down the car park. It was full of cars but, lucky for Chance, no people. Everybody was in work by nine-thirty.

The van stopped. Derek got out with a tight little knot of fear somewhere in his belly. A year ago he'd never stolen anything in his life. Then he went to work for Mr Chance, and here he was lifting a Yamaha 250 in broad daylight!

He opened the back doors and put the plank in place. His throat was dry. He wanted to cough, but didn't dare make a sound.

What if somebody saw them? Derek wondered whether the few extra quid in his pocket was worth the strain of it all. Not that he had any choice. He'd lose his job if he didn't help. Get the boot. Then what would he do?

Chance had already bypassed the safety systems of the Yamaha. He ran it up the plank.

Give me a push!

The back wheel bumped off the plank into the van, where Chance let the bike fall on its side. Derek flung in the plank and slammed the back doors shut.

The van was on the move before he'd made it into the front seat. The fear was still there in his gut as they drove back to the garage.

Back at the garage they had three hours of hard work
ahead of them. Chance took off his beard and glasses
before starting the re-spray job. The green Yamaha
became a black Yamaha with gold trim.

19

Chapter 3
Identical Dents

Caroline saw something interesting on Saturday morning.

She'd just been swimming with her brother and John. The hair dryer in the changing room didn't work, so she came outside to dry off in the warm air. Here she noticed a black Suzuki in a row of motorbikes.

For two weeks now she and the two boys had studied every Suzuki they could find. She walked over for a closer look.

There was a dent in the petrol tank of the black Suzuki.

Was it the same dent? It looked very like it. Had they been swimming in the same water as the bearded thief?

21

They decided to wait for the rider of the bike. If he turned up with a beard and a red and yellow crash helmet, they would know for sure.

But first, they let the air out of the front tyre. This was to stop the man from just riding away.

The man who came for the bike didn't have a beard, and his helmet was black. When he saw his flat tyre he gave it a kick. Caroline didn't like the look of his thick neck, or the tattooed snakes creeping from under the cuffs of his jacket. She hated tattoos. The thought of all those needle pricks made her flesh creep.

23

The man stopped pushing his bike, and scowled at them. "A beard? What's all this about? Maybe you'd like to know what I had for breakfast as well? Beat it!"

Away he went, pushing the bike up the road on his own. We should have let down *both* his tyres, Caroline thought.

But now they had some information. Bill went into a telephone booth, and sure enough, there he found what he was looking for.

What should they do now? It was quite a tricky problem. They couldn't rush off to the police with a tall story about identical dents. Anyway, the man was gone now, and so was the bike.

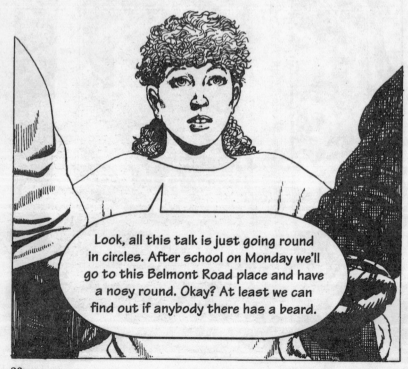

Chapter 4
Lucky Day

Raymond Chance drove the grey van along a quiet lane. He drove slowly. From time to time he glanced out of the window, because he was looking for number 14.

Most of the houses were empty during the day. Mothers and fathers worked and the kids were at school. It was a rich area. The houses were huge. And big houses meant big money.

Chance stopped the van near the front door. Then he knocked on the door – just in case. If anybody answered, he planned to say that they were selling garden furniture.

Derek sat in the van. He was glad of the ring of trees round the edge of the property. At least no one could see them from the road.

He didn't like the quiet – like the dark, it seemed to hide things. Everything he saw gave him the feeling that he should not be here.

Derek saw Mr Chance throw up the door of the garage, and wave at him. He reversed the van so that it was half in, half out, of the garage.

The motorbike sitting in the middle of the floor was a beauty.

The old Norton was a heavy machine, so they had to work hard to get it into the van. Just as the job was done, they heard a noise at the side door. They saw an old woman standing there, looking right at them.

Derek couldn't have been more terrified if she had been a ghost.

Chance grabbed a small chair and pushed the old woman into it. She sat down, quiet as a mouse, staring ahead – terrified.

Only one thought ran through Derek's mind: she's seen us, she'll know us, she'll tell on us. But why didn't she say anything? Why didn't she cry out as Mr Chance tied her to the chair with electric cable?

Now listen, granny, nobody's going to hurt you. Just sit there nice and quiet and everything will be all right.

35

But Raymond Chance was wrong. A young person with a strong heart can stand being tied up; an old person is different.

An old person like Mrs Irvine was very different. Her heart wasn't that strong. The shock of seeing two men in her son's garage was too much for her. Alone, in the cold, gloomy garage she started to panic. Frantically she struggled to free her arms and, as she struggled, her heart beat faster and faster – too fast for a woman as old as she was.

By the time the grey van got back to the garage, Mrs Irvine was dead.

Chapter 5
You go in First

Caroline, Bill and John didn't go straight home after school on Monday. They took a bus to where the bridge crossed the river near the big gas-holder. This ugly thing marked the start of Belmont Road.

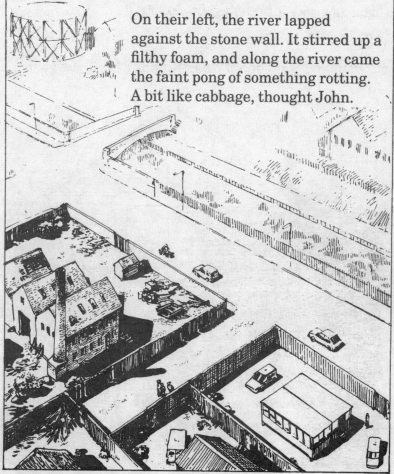

On their left, the river lapped against the stone wall. It stirred up a filthy foam, and along the river came the faint pong of something rotting. A bit like cabbage, thought John.

The garage was hard to find, but at last they spotted it at the far end of a narrow street.

The gate was closed when they arrived there. You couldn't see over the fence and there wasn't even a crack to spy through.

Then John noticed a small side door. It squeaked open when he pushed it.

"Here's a way in! Who's going in first?"

"You," said Caroline.

"Not likely!" said John. "It's *your* dad's bike, *you* go in first."

Bill pushed the door. It opened a little further, but he couldn't bring himself to go through just yet. What would they say? They had to have a reason for being here.

Bill didn't feel like laughing as he walked into the garage. Bits of bikes lay scattered over an open yard. And he saw a grey van parked near a heap of gravel.

The garage itself seemed to be made of wooden planks, like a large garden shed. There didn't seem to be anyone around.

Caroline cleared her throat.

"Excuse me. Is anybody here?" she said.

No answer.

Should they take a look round? After a moment, Caroline walked forward. It made no sense to come all this way and do nothing.

The smell of stale engine fumes lingered within the shed. Here too bits of old machines lay in jumbled piles, although the workbench was tidy.

At eye-level Caroline saw a mirror hanging on the wall. In this mirror she saw a figure in the doorway, watching her.

Spinning round, seeing him really there, Caroline felt as though her heart would stop. She wanted to run, but she knew she couldn't. Her legs wouldn't work.

The boys had seen him too. They stood like dummies in a shop window, waiting for something to happen.

At least he hasn't got a beard, thought Bill.

The man picked up a long spanner, and slapped his palm with it.

"Our dad needs a part for his bike," Caroline said with a rush.

"A clutch cable," said Bill. "It's his birthday."

The man came closer, looking from one to the other. "A clutch cable. You want a clutch cable for your dad's birthday. What kind little hearts! Now why do I have trouble believing that load of rubbish? You're in my yard to see what you can *pinch*!"

Suddenly, there was a wild shout from outside the shed. The man tossed the spanner to the floor, and went outside.

A second man – much younger – had come into the yard, and the two were arguing. The young one looked as pale as a ghost as he hammered at a newspaper with his finger. Then he ran out of the yard, leaving the small side door swinging open.

"Those two are crazy," said Bill.
"Let's get out of here."

During that sudden, mad dash across the yard on flying feet, Caroline still had time to notice something that seemed very strange. The man called Raymond Chance hardly seemed to see them go. He stood staring at the fence as if mesmerised by the shape of a particular knot of wood.

Something, she felt sure, had knocked the fight clean out of him.

Chapter 6
Follow that Boiler Suit!

Down by the river, they stopped running.

"Take your time, take your time," said John. "My legs think they're pipe cleaners. I thought we were goners back there. Did you see the size of that spanner?"

Bill gave a donkey laugh out of sheer relief. "Goldilocks and the two bears! I wonder what spooked them? That other fellow looked like he'd seen his own ghost."

Keep your voice down. He's just in front of us.

No more than a lamppost away, the fellow from the garage – still carrying his newspaper – was walking along the middle of the pavement, without looking to the left or to the right. He made strange movements with his hands, as if talking to himself, and at one point he rolled the paper into a baton and thrashed a bus stop with it.

Caroline was sure that something was worrying him.

50

At the far end of the bridge the young man suddenly threw his newspaper over the wall as if he never wanted to see it again.

"A woman found dead in her son's garage was today named as Mrs Veronica Irvine. She was 73. Police say she may have surprised thieves who made off with a motorcycle from the garage. Mrs Irvine, who was staying with her son after an illness, had been tied up in a chair. Her death is being treated as murder. Police are trying to trace a grey van seen in the area."

A chill wind swept along the river, bringing out goosepimples on Caroline's arms. She remembered the van in the yard.

"That van – what colour was it?" she said.

"Grey," said Bill.

"Or was it black?" asked John.

"It was *grey*," said Bill. "This all fits, it's the same man. He goes round the country lifting motorbikes and now he's killed somebody. We'd better figure out what to do. Let's go home and see what dad says."

Caroline stuck the paper into her pocket and followed the boys to the bus stop. She couldn't help thinking about that old lady tied up in her own garage. Suddenly the blue Suzuki didn't seem so important any more.

Back home, their dad phoned the police. He said they might have stumbled on something serious. After setting down the phone, he didn't speak for a moment or two.

"Well, that's that. It seems they're coming round to see you."

"Oh no!" said Caroline. "What if they think we're making it all up?"

"Somehow I don't think so," their dad said thoughtfully. "The officer I spoke to won't even wait for you to come to the station. There'll be a car at the front door in five minutes!"

Chapter 7
Deadly Dream

Raymond Chance stared across the dark waters of the river. The hardest thing of all was not to think.

His mind kept going back to those few moments in that garage when his world had suddenly been turned upside down. Why had he tied up that old woman? They'd have got clean away before she ever got near a phone.

How was I to know she had a dodgy heart?

He began to walk, wondering about Derek. Would Derek go to the police? Yes, yes of course he would, he would tell all. The kid had gone off his head once he'd read that paper.

Behind him he could see the sign above his garage.
RAYMOND CHANCE: QUALITY USED
MOTORCYCLES. He could hardly bear to look at it.

I only tied her up. I didn't mean her any harm.

Night was falling over the dreary river. Sunken
streetlights flickered like drowning rainbows in the
flow of ink. His dream was over, turned sour, turned
deadly. He might never ride a racing machine again.
The lights of a car came slowly down Belmont Road
and he wondered if he should run.

No point. Best to get it over with.

The car stopped and two men got out.

Still the policemen did not answer. One of them tapped the driver and the car moved off.

Chapter 8
Suzuki, Goodbye

Some days later there was a knock at the door. It was the man from the swimming baths – Caroline recognised his tattoos immediately.

He was there about the Suzuki. He hadn't known it was stolen and the police had told him to sort something out with the owner.

Caroline and Bill raced to tell John the latest news. Then they walked back to see the bike.

They were too late. At the house they were just in time to see the bike disappear round the corner. They had seen the last of it.

"Bye-bye, Suzuki," said Bill. "I wonder what that man Chance is doing right now? He's going to have plenty of time to grow a real beard."

"I wonder about the one in the boiler suit," said John. "He wasn't that old, you know. You have to feel a bit sorry for him."

Perhaps, thought Caroline. But the one she really felt sorry for was Mrs Irvine.